The German Town
and
Skippack

Jenkin's Tavern

Abingdon Meeting

K. L. J
FA

Old York Road

N

The Market Square

Cousin Hannah's

Stentor

SKIPPACK SCHOOL

Books by

MARGUERITE DE ANGELI

BLACK FOX OF LORNE

BOOK OF NURSERY AND MOTHER GOOSE RHYMES

BRIGHT APRIL

COPPER-TOED BOOTS

THE DOOR IN THE WALL

ELIN'S AMERIKA

JUST LIKE DAVID

THE OLD TESTAMENT

PETITE SUZANNE

A POCKET FULL OF POSIES

SKIPPACK SCHOOL

A SUMMER DAY WITH TED AND NINA

TED AND NINA HAVE A HAPPY RAINY DAY

TED AND NINA GO TO THE GROCERY STORE

THEE, HANNAH!

UP THE HILL

YONIE WONDERNOSE

Skippack School

eing the story of Eli Shrawder and of one Christopher Dock, schoolmaster about the year 1750

By Marguerite de Angeli

Doubleday and Company, Inc.

To My
Mother

REE-EE-K! CREE-EE-K!" The wheels of the cart groaned and squeaked as they turned round and round over the rough block pavement on High Street in Philadelphia. They went up past the Court House, then turned off onto the road that led out into Penn's Woods and through the German Town.

To Eli it seemed as if he could still feel the roll of the ship beneath him. He and his father and mother, Peter and Catherine Shrawder, and his two little sisters had landed early that morning. They had crossed the ocean in the ship called *The Charming Nancy* and had been ten long weeks on the ocean. Eli shivered as he remembered the storm at sea that made them all ill, and the terror that came over him when giant waves rolled the boat and the chests and boxes slid from one side to the other of the cabin floor.

He was glad to be on land, with the fresh country air to sniff. It was good! The wagon creaked on and on, out through the deep woods.

"It wonders me now," said Pop, "that the houses stand so close in Penn's green country town."

"Yah," said Mom, "like a city it vas, but *here* iss nice!"

Cousin Jacob called back to them.

"Soon now," he said, "we come to the German Town." Cousin Jacob rode ahead on horseback. He and Cousin Hannah had lived in the German Town for several years and he had come down to meet the ship and help Pop buy a wagon to take them and their few pieces of furniture to the land out in the newer settlement beyond the German Town. Buck and Berry, the oxen, and Star, the cow, had come with them across the ocean.

"Over there by the Wissahickon Creek iss Rittenhouse's paper mill. Good paper he makes." Cousin Jacob pointed to his left. Eli had never seen a paper mill. It sounded exciting. He wished he could see it but he could find no sign of the mill through the thick woods, only the trail leading toward it.

Slowly the wagon creaked over the deep ruts in the road. Oxen always move slowly and besides, Star, the cow, was tethered to the back of the cart; but by noon they got to the German Town and there was Cousin Hannah to greet them. She came out the gate and helped them to climb down from the wagon: Sibilla, then Eli, then Mom. "Ach!" she said in German, "so tired you must be! And the *little* one." She took the tiny babe from Mom and led them into the house.

After a bountiful dinner in Cousin Jacob's fine house, they set out again in the wagon. Cousin Hannah tucked in a basket filled with good things. She had a box of live geese ready, too. They tied it on the back of the wagon.

"Something, now, to begin with," she said. And she and Cousin Jacob stood at the gate and waved good-by as they started off.

It was market day and the street was filled with people on horseback and afoot. The sides of the street were lined with wagons and with food stalls. Eli even saw two or three of the Indians he had heard about. Cousin Jacob had said they were all friendly because William Penn had treated them with such fairness. Eli longed to see them better, but Pop wouldn't stop. He was eager to get to their land.

The afternoon wore on. Cree-ee-k! Cree-ee-k! went the wagon wheels.

It seemed to Eli as if he had heard that squeaking, grinding noise for weeks.

"Is it soon, Pop, that we come to the place?" he asked.

"Yah, soon," said Pop, as they passed a little church that stood away up on the hill. "This is the wide marsh, where the other road comes in. Skeback, or Skippack, or some such, Jacob said. It wonders me if we get there by nightfall."

"It gives a long journey," said Mom, and sighed. Then she took a deep breath. "It gives a good smell, too, and room for growing, ain't?"

Eli sat between Pop and Mom. Sibilla, his little sister, who was four, sat on Mom's lap. The baby, Barbara Ann, was asleep in her cradle in the back

of the cart. She had been born aboard ship coming across the Atlantic Ocean from Holland, where they had waited so long for word about the land Pop had bought from Cousin Jacob.

The Shrawders and many other families had left Germany together to find new homes where they could worship God in their own way. They called themselves Mennonites after their leader, Menno Simons. They dressed "plain" like the English Friends who had already come to Pennsylvania. The men

14

even had hooks and eyes to fasten their vests instead of buttons. The women wore plain dark dresses and white kerchiefs and caps. They had gone first to Holland, where they stayed for a time, but there they heard such glowing reports of the new land in America from Cousin Jacob and others who had settled in Penn's Woods, they had set out to find it.

"So to Pennsylvanie, then, we shall go," said Pop one day. But it had been many months before they could get passage on a boat to the new world. Already the home life in Germany was so far away that it seemed like a dream. Pop said there were many Germans along the Skippack Creek in Pennsylvania near where they were going and in the village called Skippack, so it would be a little like home.

Now they were almost there. Eli looked up through the great trees, so much like the ones he remembered in Germany. The woods were full of the songs of birds; squirrels and small animals of all kinds crossed the wagon trail, and the land seemed full of plenty.

They had passed few houses since leaving the German Town, but finally they came to a tavern. Pop said:

"Now we are near to our land. Here we stay for the night."

Mom, the baby and Sibilla had a great double bed in one of the rooms of the Swan Tavern kept by Gerrit Inden Hoffen, but Pop made a place in the wagon and said to Eli, "We can sleep here and save the cost of another room."

Early the next morning they set out again. Smoke was just beginning to rise from the chimneys of the few farmhouses they passed. But by the time

they reached the village store it was open, and a little boy was sweeping off the steps.

He stared curiously at the wagon, then ran inside and they heard him calling, "Oh, Pop, the new neighbors it must be."

The storekeeper hurried out to greet them, smiling a welcome.

"Yah, Jacob was right. He sent word last week only that he was sure your ship would be in within a few days. And a good time it is too, for the building. The spring planting is finished, everyone will be ready to start today."

Cousin Jacob had told Pop that it was the custom in Penn's Woods for the neighbors to gather and help cut the trees and build the cabin whenever new settlers arrived. And now the storekeeper was explaining that he would send word to all the farmers.

"Right ahead you go, into the woods past Eidmuller's farm," he directed. "Nice land, you have, and soon a new home. We start with the building today."

The woods were still cool when they passed the great butternut tree that marked the corner of their land. Eli had been watching for the tree. It was shown on the map of the land Cousin Jacob had given Pop.

He shouted with excitement when he saw it—but Pop didn't stop. They drove on more slowly until they found a slight clearing in the woods.

"This makes a good home place," Pop said. Mom nodded agreement and Eli and Sibby jumped off the wagon and ran happily through the woods, glad to be once more on land.

Pop had hardly picked out the spot for the house before the first farmer arrived. It was Jonas Eidmuller whose farm bordered the Shrawders' land.

"Soon, now, the others will come," he said. "To set the posts for the house *now* vas *gut!* The moon stands up *so* and dey vill shtay." He held up his two forefingers to show how the moon stood.

Eli knew the old belief among the Germans that fence posts or buildings must be set in the ground only when the crescent moon was on its back, or the ground would be soggy and the posts would not be solid.

"Und soon now iss the time for planting beans," Jonas Eidmuller continued. "Nex' week iss gut. It iss de sign of the twins in de almanac. You plant den and dey grow *plenty* und *big* too!"

One by one the farmers came: some in wagons, some afoot. Their wives came too, and each family had food for themselves and to spare. They brought great kettles and put them up with chains on three poles set together.

While the men chopped down trees, the women cooked. They cooked food Eli had never tasted before. Corn meal, scrapple and pepper pot. The babies were put to sleep in the wagons, and the young children, who didn't go to school, gathered small wood for the fires and played with the babies when they waked. It was like a festival, Eli thought. When school was over, some of the older children came to watch and to be with their parents.

Everyone worked hard. A sharp ax and good strong muscles were needed to chop down the big trees, but they were so large that it didn't take a great many to build the house. There were stones in a near-by quarry to use for the chimney and springs of clear water close at hand. No wonder the reports of Penn's Woods had traveled so far!

Eli was allowed to trim off some of the branches as the trees came down and he felt it was much more fun than anything he had ever done.

After the branches were cut off, each log was trimmed with the adz and cut at the ends to fit so that there wouldn't be too much space between them to be chinked with mud. When night came, some of the farmers and their families went home, and some slept in the wagons.

The next day everyone was up early. Eli fed the animals. Then Pop told him to help Jonas Eidmuller, who was splitting shingles for the roof.

"Yah, sure you can help," Jonas said. "In piles by the walls they should

go, so it makes easier when they start the roofing. That's a good boy."

Eli made many trips with the shingles—and in between times he rested a bit and listened to Jonas Eidmuller, who was a great talker.

"So," he said, "you like this new home, yes?" Eli nodded.

"And soon," Jonas continued, "you will be off to school with the other young ones. That you will like too, eh? Master Christopher Dock makes a fine school here on the Skippack."

This time Eli didn't nod. School was the one thing he didn't like about this new home. He had gone to school only a few months in Germany—and he had hated being shut in. He hadn't learned much either—not even all of his letters because he didn't pay attention. The schoolmaster was cross and had even sent a note home, complaining of his mischief and lack of attention.

Mom had worried about it. On the ship she had tried teaching Eli his letters, but there were always interruptions. She had told Eli he must do better in the new home. And Eli had promised to be good and work hard —but he still wasn't happy about school.

By the third night the roof of the new cabin was on. All the farmers and their families went back to their homes, and Pop and Eli moved in the furniture they had brought across the ocean. Mom was as pleased as she could be with the wide fireplace, its iron crane for pots and kettles, and the oven at one end. The floor, made of short pieces of log set on end, formed a pattern of circles. It smelled clean and fresh and it was solid to step upon.

Next day, Mom's and Pop's bed was built into a corner of the room, and the curtains brought from the homeland were put up. Eli's bed, made of stout pine logs with the bark peeled off, was set up in the loft. Sibilla's trundle-bed was there too, and Eli cut fresh pine branches to put under the feather ticks. Sibilla brought her little play cupboard and chair and put them in the chimney corner. Pop set the clock between the windows, and Mom put the spinning wheel close by.

"It makes not much furniture," said Mom, as she hung the house blessing over the front door.

"Ach," said Pop, as he moved the painted chest against the far wall, "soon we make more! Some wide boards iss left from the door-making, und Eli helps good with a saw and plane. We soon make a table and other things. Eli, here, thinks he can make a bench for you to put in front of the fireplace. Already, a good board he has found."

There was much laughing and happy talk as they put the wash bench by the back door, and Mom hung up her pots and kettles by the fireplace. Then Pop laid the fire for supper. *It was home!*

OR A WEEK, Eli helped Pop clear the space around the house and set things in order. They made a table and built a small shelter for the cattle and fixed a workbench and a place for Pop's tools. And, whenever he had a minute, Eli worked on the fireplace bench. It was a good piece of pine, Pop said, and not to be wasted. He showed Eli how to use the plane to smooth it and helped him make the holes for the end pieces.

Eli worked carefully—but he could hardly wait to get the thick board smooth enough so he could begin on the carving. It was to have a carved border, as nearly like the one on a little bench Mom's brother had made for her, in Germany, as Eli could make it. Mom had hated to leave the bench, but they could not bring everything they wanted so far across the ocean.

Eli remembered every detail of the border. And he loved to carve. He had his own knife, one his uncle had given him so he shouldn't forget his wood carving in Penn's Woods. But for the bench Pop said he would have to use the small chisel.

Mom was pleased about the bench, too. Eli hoped that she would forget about school until he had finished it. But when Sunday came she said firmly, "Now to school you must go."

The next morning Pop took Eli to the bend in the road and told him to follow the path. It would lead him to the schoolhouse that stood beside the log Mennonite Church where several trails came together.

Eli stopped to shy a stone at a scampering woodchuck. He missed it. Mr. Woodchuck scuttled under the leaves of an oak seedling, then he was gone. Eli looked and looked but couldn't find where. He picked up his lunch basket and went on his way to school. . . . School! How he dreaded to go to school in this new place! It was so much more fun to chase squirrels in the woods or go fishing or work on Mom's bench.

He dragged his feet through cool leaves and grass, looked up through the tall trees and wished he could stay at home, even if it meant working in the fields, chopping wood for Mom; yes, even if it meant minding the baby in her cradle! *Any*thing would be better than going to this new school! "Probably," he thought, "the schoolmaster will be ugly and cross."

Eli heard the bell ringing and began to run. In just a moment the trees thinned a bit, and he came out in a little clearing. There stood the school and the church just as Pop had said. The boys and girls were all going in, but instead of pushing and crowding as Eli remembered their doing in the other school, they were walking in two by two, the boys waiting until last. He hurried a little faster in order not to be late; he didn't want a caning the very first day!

He came up to the door as the last two boys were going in. Just then the schoolmaster came to the door.

"Come, come, boys! What is keeping you?" he asked. Then he spied Eli. "So," he said, "a new *boy* we have! Come in, Sir." He took Eli by the hand and led him to the front of the room.

"It wonders me what he is going to do to me!" Eli thought. His heart beat fast. He saw two or three boys who had been to the log raising, Amos and Reuben and a little girl named Anneke—but still he felt strange.

"Now," said the schoolmaster, "I am Master Christopher Dock, and these are all your friends. Will you tell us your name?"

Eli's throat was very dry, but he managed to say, "Eli Shrawder, Sir."

"Eli Shrawder! Then you are the boy who lives in that new house. Boys and girls stand up and greet Eli!" They all stood up, and the boys made bows and the girls curtsied.

"Now," said Master Christopher, "you may sit there on the bench beside Amos Freyer. Make room for him, Amos." Eli sat down on the bench. The desks and benches were around the walls, facing outward; the

boys sat on one side of the room, the girls on the other. The schoolmaster sat at a desk on the little platform at the front of the room. On the desk were inkstand, sand box, and quill pen; several books beside the Bible, and some field flowers in a vase. Eli saw that the schoolmaster had a birch rod up on the pegs at one side where it was handy, and on the other side, a rifle in its rack. It was warm enough for the windows to be open, so there was no

need for a fire in the ten-plate stove that stood in the middle of the room. All the children were neat and clean, Eli noticed, and when Master Christopher spoke to them, they were very respectful.

"Eli Shrawder," said the master when the first class went to the platform, "do you know your letters?"

"Some," said Eli.

"Eli, when you speak to me, say: 'Yes, Master Christopher.' That is the proper way to answer any man, and not because especial respect is due *me*."

This time Eli said, "Yes, Master Christopher, I know some of the letters." Then he had to take the pointer and point out what he knew. He was a little ashamed that he didn't know more, when Master Christopher said: "Amos, you take care to see that Eli learns his letters; then he can stand with the first class."

"Yes, Master Christopher," said Amos. The lessons went on. Amos, talking quietly, told Eli how the master helped the children to do their best. And how he often gave them presents for good work; pictures and verses called "Fractur-Schriften," because that meant picture writing. He said when they learned to write well they were allowed sometimes to write letters to the children in the German Town School, and receive letters in return. Master Christopher carried the letters back and forth. He taught the first half of the week in the Skippack School and the other half in the German Town School. So Wednesday afternoons were saved for special exercises, for spelling bees and for the giving of prizes.

When noontime came, Master Christopher said, "Now, Eliza, and you, Tobias Bean, shall have each a sugar pretzel; you have learned well today. Jacob, for your excellent attention this morning, you may read the chapter from the Old Testament while the children are eating.

"Read where it says: 'Train up a child in the way he should go and when he is old, he will not depart from it.' School is dismissed for dinner."

He struck a little bell, and the children formed two lines as they had done coming in. They filed out quietly but burst into laughter and talk for a few moments until Jacob, perched on a tree stump, began to read. Then they sat down on the grass and ate quietly.

Eli, who thought this a very tame way to spend the free time between morning and afternoon lessons, began to shy stones up into the trees. It was all very well till one of them fell on the roof; then Master Christopher came to the door. He took off his glasses and looked at all the children; then seeing Eli standing and the others sitting, he said:

"Eli Shrawder, were you throwing stones?" Eli looked into the master's eyes and said:

"Yes, Master Christopher, but it didn't hurt anybody."

"No, but you *might* and you might break the windows. That wouldn't do at all. Windows cost a great deal of money." Eli knew that, because Pop had said they would have to use oiled paper for the windows at home for a while. He said: "Yes, Master Christopher," and his face was very red because all the children were looking at him.

The afternoon went better. Eli knew the verses that had to be recited because Mom had taught them to him. He still couldn't tell many of the letters, but Master Christopher said:

"There is time for all, my boy, if only we do not waste it. If today you do not learn, but *try*, the next time it will go better."

Claus Johnson whispered to Eli, "Sometimes," he said, "Master Christopher lets me help make pencils and sometimes he takes a boy to visit the German Town School. But never have I been."

Claus whispered so often that he was made to sit on the dunce's stool the rest of the afternoon.

Finally, the master took his great silver watch out of his pocket.

"Now, Claus," he said at last, "can you be quiet tomorrow? Today you made Eli talk too. School is for learning. Do not forget! Jacob, remember to ask your mother to sew up the rent in your shirt. Sarah, dear child, see if you can read well tomorrow and remember not to twist your hair."

"Yes, Master Christopher," said Sarah, "but my hair is so stribbly."

"Reuben," said the master, as he leaned over a boy near him, "if you do well at reading this week, you will be glad when Wednesday comes." He smiled and nodded, then closed his eyes.

"Now God bless you all and bring you back safe in the morning."

The girls got up and walked out two by two; then the boys followed.

Eli could scarcely believe it. A *whole* day and not once had the schoolmaster used the birch rod! Not once had he even been angry! It ought to be easy to have fun in this school. Eli tossed his broad hat into the air.

VERY DAY after school, Eli helped Pop to hoe the beans they had planted. He had to keep the wood box filled too, and to help care for Star and the oxen. But if he hurried there was some time every day when he could work on the fireplace bench. He had the boards all planed now and had begun to fit the end pieces into the top.

Several days when Master Christopher was teaching in the German Town, and there was no school on the Skippack, Eli went with Pop to help hoe the flax in Jonas Eidmuller's field. Jonas had agreed to share his crop of flax with Pop if they would help work it. Then Mom would have linen to spin into yarn and to make into cloth for shirts and dresses.

At first Eli's arms ached from the hard work but, as the weeks passed, he became used to it and was proud of his muscles. Sometimes Pop let him go fishing with Amos and Claus in the branch that flowed through the village and into the Skippack Creek. Sometimes they slipped off their clothes and went into the water down below the mill race. It felt so cool and good!

Pop worked very hard at clearing the land so that he could plant more the next year. Eli liked that kind of work, trimming branches from trees, burning brush, guiding Buck and Berry as they dragged the stumps from the ground. The small animals they discovered as they worked supplied food for the table. Sometimes they caught wild turkeys that Mom roasted on the spit.

Mom did the milking and made the butter and cheese. She said a little rhyme as she worked the butter. It went like this:

Come, butter, come,
Come, butter, come,
Peter's waiting at the gate,
Waiting for a buttered cake,
Come, butter, come.

Mom had to dip candles too, and do the spinning and knitting. While she was busy, Sibilla played with the baby in her cradle or on a quilt under a tree.

Mom had set cabbages out in part of the space Pop cleared first, so that she could make sauerkraut for winter. Corn meal, which they had learned to like so well, and wheaten flour, they could get at Gerrit Inden Hoffen's mill.

To be sure, Pop didn't have any money left after all their journeying, but Mom had things in the painted chest that could be traded. She had steel needles, which were very scarce in the new land, and medicines given her by her father who was an apothecary in Germany. Mom also had bolts of flowered silks from her wedding dowry and these could be traded for necessities now that she and Pop had joined the "plain" people, the Mennonites.

School kept on through the summer, because in midwinter when the roads were impassable, it had to be closed.

Slowly Eli learned the capitals and small letters, but it was hard not to get them mixed. Sometimes he wondered if he could possibly learn them before school closed. It was so hard to keep his mind on letters. He sat right in front of the window and there was always something to watch outside. The blue jays were always fighting and squawking, their blue wings flashing in and out of the leaves. A family of gray squirrels raced up and down the oak tree down by the spring. Once a fox came out of the woods and stood for a moment gazing toward the schoolhouse. Eli was so surprised he stood up and stared out the window. Just then Master Christopher called on him to join the children who were going up to recite their A B C's. He had to be spoken to twice.

"Eli Shrawder," said the master, "the Book says, 'Love and not sleep, lest thou come to poverty.' "

"But, I was not asleep, Master Christopher," said Eli, "I was just wishing I could be out in the woods instead of having letters to learn."

"Your mind was asleep, my boy. How will you ever learn to read if you never keep your mind on your work?" The master looked sorrowful. "Whatever you want to do, you will find it useful to know your letters and sums."

Many times a week the master had to speak to Eli. He was either thinking up mischief or dreaming about the bench he was making at home. He had the bench together now, and it was all finished except the carving.

June passed and July came in, hot and sultry. It was almost closing time of the last school day of the week, Wednesday. Eli sat trying to puzzle out a sum of numbers. Slate pencils scratched, the droning voices of the girls learning their verses and the bench creaking when the boys wriggled added to his discomfort. The pegs holding up the bench seemed loose; Eli whispered to Amos Freyer; Amos turned and whispered something to Claus Johnson; Claus turned and whispered something to Jacob Heebner; Jacob sniggered. The master was busy with a class of girls at the board. All of a sudden there was a great clatter and crash! Master Christopher looked around in amazement. There on the floor, laughing so hard they couldn't get up, were all the boys from one form. They had wiggled at the legs of the bench till they had

all come loose and down clattered bench, boys and all. Teacher looked grave.

"Now," he said, very quietly, "since you boys are so anxious to take wood apart, you shall all stay one hour after school is over and work at the woodpile. Those logs beside the oak you shall saw and split and pile against the time we shall need them for the stove. Now put the bench together again."

Because the master was so gentle, Eli was ashamed. He almost wished he would use the birch rod instead, as he had that one time when Abel Larsen had cut his name in the desk, then lied about it.

July passed with still, hot days to make the corn grow, and thunder showers to freshen the air. August came in, and the days grew warmer and warmer. It was hard to stay in school and try to learn to read when the flies buzzed and the heat shimmered across the fields; especially when the Skippack Creek ran clear and cool not more than a half hour's walk away. Eli could feel just how soft the grass would be along the bank and kept thinking how much fun it was to make whistles of the willow shoots, or to whittle the soft white pine that grew thick in the hollows. School seemed endless and to learn letters or anything else all foolishness.

At noontime, the master gave the children some free time to play. Amos said to Eli, "Let's play 'Eckballe,' " corner ball. He showed Eli the new ball he had made of string wound tight and covered with horsehide from the tannery. He told him how to stand at the corner of the building and throw the ball across the roof to the other corner where Amos would be standing. It went over high and well above the roof the first few times. Then Eli tried to make it go higher.

He put all the strength he had into his arm. He must have turned his

arm a little because, instead of going over the roof, the ball went *right straight through the window!* Master Christopher rushed out to see who had thrown the ball. He made both Amos and Eli come in and he kept the ball. "Now," he said, "your fathers will have to see to replacing the window. 'A foolish son is a grief to his father,' so says the Book." Eli was so scared he had a queer feeling in his stomach.

When closing time came the master called out the names of several boys and girls. "Eliza, Anneke, Tobias, Jacob, come forward. Eli Shrawder, you may come, too, though you were in that mischief." They all went up to the front of the room.

Eli was sure he would be caned this time. He waited till the master spoke to each of the others.

"Eliza," he said, "you have entered the reading class. You have done well. I give you this gift." Eliza took from him the paper and smiled with pleasure. The paper had on it a painting of a bird set on a heart in which was written, "Noble Heart bethink thine end."

To Anneke the master gave one of the flower paintings and said, "Dear child, so well you are learning to write, soon you may write a letter to Esther in the German Town and I shall carry it to her."

Eli looked longingly at Anneke's flower painting. How proud Mom would be if he earned one. Every week since he had started school he had wanted one. But it was only for good work that Master Christopher awarded them—and now, Eli thought sadly, Master Christopher would never

give one to anyone who had broken a window.

"Now Eli, you know," said Master Christopher, "when you have thoroughly learned your small letters, your father owes you a penny and your mother shall cook for you two fried eggs as I have told them is my custom. You have earned this, but you have also made a great deal of mischief. So, I shall send a note with you to your father that it is time for the penny and the two fried eggs, but he shall be told also about the broken window. And from now on I shall put you in charge of Tobias, who has done well this week. We shall see if he can help you remember that school is not the place for pranks."

Eli was ashamed to be spoken to before the whole class. But he was more ashamed to have to tell Mom and Pop about the window. What would they say? Would Pop punish him?

It was time for dismissal. The master blessed them and sent them home.

Eli walked as far as the top of the hill with Claus, then went slowly on home. He dreaded to tell about the window. As soon as he reached home he went straight to the shed and began to work at the carving on the bench. The scalloped edge was fun to make and kept him busy till Mom called him to bring in the cow.

HAT EVENING after supper was over, Mom was putting Barbara Ann into her cradle, Pop was feeding the oxen, Sibilla was sitting on the doorstep and Eli was trying to get the pigs into the shed for the night. He was gathering acorns to coax them in. There was a sound of hoofs and out of the woods an Indian came riding. Eli was so surprised, he dropped the acorns and ran for the house. The pigs ran too, and the geese, waddling up from the creek, went squawking in all directions. The Indian saluted Pop who was just coming out of the barn, but he didn't stop. He kept on toward the west and was soon lost in the woods again. It was the first time Eli had seen an Indian that close.

"It wonders me," said Pop, "what it makes that an Indian goes by alone and didn't stop to eat. Ach! Vell, Jacob says they make no trouble here. *So!*" He went to get the grinder he was making and called to Eli to find the pigs again.

"Now come, Eli," he called, when the pigs and geese were put in the shed, "and let me see how good you can make the capital letters. Right here in the ground where the earth iss hard, you can make them with a stick." Mom came out with her knitting and they worked in the evening light.

"Now," thought Eli, "I shall *have* to tell about the window." He stood first on one foot, then the other, and made no attempt to begin on the letters.

"What makes," said Pop, "that you stand and wiggle so?" He looked into Eli's face.

"Ach *so!*" he said. "I see by your eyes that somesing makes wrong. What iss it?"

Then Eli gave Pop the master's note and told him about playing corner ball with Amos and how, without meaning to, he had thrown the ball right through the window.

"Tch! Tch! said Pop. "Now what shall be done? Windows cost money, and you should know to be careful." He sat and thought. Mom dropped her knitting and said, "The painted chest might have something we could sell, maybe."

"*Eli* should have to pay," said Pop. "He ought to learn to be careful. That bench, now, that he makes, nobody here would buy it, but maybe in

the German Town it would sell. Amos he should help, too."

"Oh, no," cried Eli, "the bench, it is for Mom"—and then he stopped. Mom looked sorry, but Pop was shaking his head firmly.

"Yes, the bench I could trade, maybe. When it is finished I will try in the German Town."

Eli was miserable. To trade Mom's bench for glass! Oh, why had he ever thrown that ball? For the rest of the week he couldn't even work on the bench he was so disappointed. But on Monday it did help to tell Master Christopher what Pop had said.

"Yes, that is good, my child, perhaps you can sell the bench before the cold weather comes," the master told him. "You and Amos may help me this noontime to put paper over the broken place until we can mend it."

That day Eli tried so hard and made his letters so well, that Master Christopher said, "Eli, today you may stay and help me make lead pencils." Eli was delighted. They heated lead on the little stove, then poured it into the cracks of the floor. When it was cool, they dug it out with a knife, and the hard lead made good clear marks on paper. The schoolmaster noticed how interested Eli was in making things.

"I can see thee likes to use thy hands, Eli," he said, "but to know the letters and the sums is good too, and needful. Keep trying hard, dear child, and keep thyself from mischief. The Book says, 'He that keepeth himself, is greater than he that taketh a city.' "

Eli did try hard but, always, something seemed to happen. At home he could work steadily for hours, carving the fireplace bench. In school he just couldn't keep his mind on lessons and then he got into mischief. If the tiny children sat on the low bench near him, he couldn't seem to help pinching little Nancy's fat neck and making her cry, or pulling Catherine's curls from under her cap.

Master Christopher kept him after school again and talked to him a long time. Eli promised to keep from mischief, and he really meant to, but only a few days later when they were singing the morning hymn, he thought of a play rhyme he remembered from Germany and he went on singing the rhyme instead of the hymn. The rhyme was funny and made him laugh, so that he had to stop singing altogether. The master only said:

" 'A word fitly spoken is like apples of gold in pictures of silver.' Begin the hymn again."

At recess, Amos showed Eli a fan he had made by soaking a piece of soft pine and splitting it in thin blades part way down, then spreading the pieces in fanshape. Eli was supposed to be learning the verse put up before him on the wall but instead he had been thinking of the scalloped edge he was carving on the bench, and how nice it looked. Now the idea occurred to him that he could make a fan for Mom. It would be something in place of the bench. The fan would be pretty, too, with a pattern cut across the sticks.

"Mom would like a fan like that," he thought. He took his knife out of his pocket and a stick that he kept for whittling, just to try and see how it looked. He cut little notches along the edge to form a diamond pattern and

45

was just about to carve a design on the other side, when the master called to him.

"Eli, is it that you know so much that you have time for play? 'Folly is joy to him that is destitute of wisdom.' Your exercise must be well learned, so you may stand for questioning."

"Yes, Master Christopher," said Eli, getting to his feet, but he trembled because he didn't know the verse. He was sure Master Christopher would cane him this time!

"Eli," said the master, "what is the verse you have had before you all morning." All the girls and boys turned in their seats to look at him and the master took off his spectacles and looked severe.

Eli tried and tried to think what was on that paper that had been hanging before him on the wall, but not a word would come to him. He hung his head.

"Aren't you ashamed?" said the teacher. "Now you are to listen with care and know this before the hour to go home. Jacob, let us hear the exercise." Master Christopher put on his spectacles again and folded his hands behind him.

Jacob was able to say the exercise with only one mistake. Then Sarah was asked to say it. She knew it perfectly but rattled it off too quickly.

Master was very patient. He corrected each one, then gave Eli one more chance to say the verse. Eli knew some of it but he hadn't learned it perfectly, so he was made to stay after the others had gone and study until he knew every word. Then Master Christopher said he might go. Eli was so glad to be free, that he was almost home before he remembered his lunch basket. He had to go back for it and he hurried, hoping the master hadn't left and locked the door. Knowing Master Christopher's habit of study and prayer after the children had gone, Eli went softly over the doorstep and lifted the latch carefully.

There was Master Christopher on his knees, his eyes closed and praying aloud.

"And Eli Shrawder, O Lord, he is not a *bad* boy, but he is so full of mischief. Help me to show him how to use his time aright. He has a sweet singing voice too, but thou knowest that sometimes he uses that voice to say mischief——"

Eli didn't wait to hear any more. He tiptoed out and left his basket. Something rose up in his throat and almost choked him. He ran into the woods and threw himself down. "I must be very wicked," he thought to himself. Then he was afraid someone, perhaps the master, might see him, so he got up, rubbed his eyes and ran for home. He *would* stop making mischief! He *would* earn one of those bird paintings for Mom.

LL THROUGH the rest of the summer and through September Eli tried very hard to keep his mind on his school work, and Master Christopher seemed pleased about it.

One evening, after supper, Eli asked Mom to hear him read. She wondered why he was suddenly taking so much interest in reading, but she said nothing and just helped him over the hard words. Pop came in from the barn and heard him.

"Yah!" he said. "Good! Good! The little one has learned pat-a-cake, Sibby learns to knit, and *you*, now, *can read!* Tomorrow, you can read the Book, for morning prayers."

Pop always read the Scriptures. Eli was very proud. Now, perhaps, Master Christopher would let him read it in school. If he did it well, the master would surely give him a present of a flower or bird picture.

The next morning, Eli read the Psalm as Pop had promised. Pop had to help him a little, but he did it very well. He hurried to school as soon as breakfast was over, and that day the lesson went so smoothly for him that the teacher said:

"Now, my child, tomorrow you will be able to read the morning Scriptures. You are doing well, Eli. But the Book says, 'Boast not thyself of tomorrow; for thou knowest not what a day may bring forth.'"

Eli knew how glad Mom would be. He could hardly wait to tell her. He wanted to get home and work a little more on the bench before he began the afternoon chores. The carving was done and ready for finishing with the pumice rubbing stone.

Now that the flax was gathered, Eli had to work every afternoon at the flax brake. It was a large double frame of wood, hinged at the back. The stalks of flax were laid between the top and bottom frames, then when the top came down, it broke away the woody stems and left the soft part. After the flax was hackled and combed, Mom heaped it on the spindle for spinning into yarn. Already, much of it was done, and Mom kept the spinning wheel whirring all day long. Eli had taken some of the yarn she had spun and dyed to Andris Souplis, the weaver in the village, who made it into brown and white checked linen cloth. Some of the cloth Mom kept to

make into shirts for Pop and for Eli. Some of it Eli had taken to the village store to sell. He liked making the bargain with the storekeepers, seeing the people in the village and hearing Jonas Eidmuller say:

"Geese down makes thick, und squirrel tail makes bushy, *so* a hard vinter comes—ain't?"—or: "Thick shucks on de corn, and leaves from de trees come off from de tops first, *so* lots of schnow und ice dis vinter, think?"

Mom knew he liked taking the yarn to the village and selling the linen at the store, but she said:

"The letters you must know and how to do sums, or how can you tell what is right to get for the linen? A smart boy knows how to read too."

When he reached home, Mom said, "Get right now to work at the flax. My spindle is empty and only a little iss left in the barn ready for the hackle." So there was no time to do any work on the bench after all, but Mom was pleased when Eli told her that he was to read the Scriptures at the opening of school in the morning.

As he worked Eli thought, "I will read so well tomorrow, Master Christopher will give me a beautiful picture I can give to Mom." All afternoon Eli slammed the flax brake up and down. He didn't stop except for the time it took to bring Star from the pasture down by the Skippack. Pop kept her in the shed at night, now that the frost had come.

When Eli had a bundle of flax ready for the hackle, he took it into the barn, and threw it down on a pile in the corner. He wasn't anxious to get back to the flax brake. He stood for a moment, watching Star who stood in the stall chewing her cud. Everything was so still! Except for Star's munching, there wasn't a sound.

"It wonders me now," Eli thought, "did ever a cow jump over the moon? What would a cow look like if she could dance?" Star stood perfectly still chewing her cud. Eli's eyes wandered to the oxgoad that hung beside the bin.

"It wonders me, what would Star do if I should juu-usst *touch* her with that." He lifted the goad down and tiptoed over to Star's stall. He flicked gently at Star's round side with the tip of the goad. She moved suddenly to one side. Eli chuckled. He tried it again. She danced! Then he struck her again, this time on the flank and a bit harder. Star fairly pranced! Eli was filled with delight. He lifted the goad and brought it down smartly over Star's back. She lifted her dainty hoofs clear of the floor, her tail swung up, and she *moo*ed. This was fun! Next, Eli laid the switch on still harder, and right where the flesh was most tender. Star plunged and pranced. She bellowed in fright and pain—*but—so—did—Eli!!* Pop had come in. Taking Eli by the shirt band and trousers, he lifted him clear of the floor. Then Pop took the oxgoad and laid it on where he thought it would do the most good. "Now," Pop said, "into the house you go and to bed."

Mom looked up in surprise but said nothing as Eli went up the stairs.

Eli undressed and lay down. He couldn't sleep. He lay for a long time awake and miserable. It hurt where Pop had whipped him, but it hurt more inside when he thought that maybe Pop would send word to Master Christopher, and he wouldn't be allowed to read the Scriptures the next day. Finally, he went to sleep.

It was still black dark when he heard Pop go out to hitch up Buck and Berry for market, and not quite light when he was awakened again by a loud knocking, and Mom calling, from the bed corner.

"Eli, Eli, come! Somesing makes by the door, and Pop's gone by the German Town." The pounding on the door kept up, and a voice called, "Mrs. Shrawder, Mrs. Shrawder!" So Mom wrapped a bed quilt around her, hurried to light a candle and went to the door. The baby began to cry, and Sibilla woke up to see what was the matter. Before Eli could get into his trousers and down the ladder Mom lifted the bar from the door and opened the upper half. There stood Katie Kreider all out of breath, her face white and drawn. When Mom saw who it was, she opened the lower half of the door and Katie came in.

"Margareth's taken bad with her foot again. She stepped on a rusty nail, and the nail we greased and hung it in the chimbly, like our mother used to do, but now she is bad again; the foot as big as a barrel." Mom didn't waste time in talking. She put the candle down. Then she dressed behind the bed curtains, fed the crying baby and wrapped her up warmly to be taken

along. She went to the painted chest, gathered up her herbs and some pieces of flannel and put them into a little cloth bag that she carried on her arm.

Katie lived with her sister down the road and back through the forest. Her sister Margareth's husband had bought the land there and begun to clear it but had been killed by a falling tree. Now the two sisters lived alone and found it hard to run a farm in the wilderness without a man to help. Mom had been a friend to them in their trouble as she was to many others and, because she knew something of medicines and herbs, was called upon to help where there was sickness. Often Mom was called out in the middle of the night, but Pop had always been there before to look after the children.

"Na come, Katie," said Mom, "you carry these flannels. Eli," she called over her shoulder, "Sibby you must care for till I come back. Sleep now." Blowing out the candle, Mom took the baby, went out after Katie and closed the door. Sibilla wailed. Eli lay down beside her on the pallet. He comforted her as best he could with nursery rhymes, and soon they were both asleep.

THE SUN coming through a crack in the logs woke Eli. The morning felt strange. There was no smell of breakfast, no warmth of a fire, no sound of the baby nor of Mom moving about. Then he remembered. Mom had gone with Katie before daylight and she wasn't back yet. Eli crept down the ladder to look at the tall clock. It was almost time for school! School! And he was to read the Scriptures and perhaps get a present from Master Christopher! But he couldn't go to school and leave Sibilla alone! He couldn't take her to school either. It was too far. He had looked forward to this day for so long. Now he wouldn't get the present for reading well. He stood looking at the clock—it ticked slowly on.

Sibilla woke up. He ran up the ladder and helped her to dress, then put on his own clothes. Sibilla wanted her breakfast, so he tried to hurry. One stocking went on wrong side out. That meant good luck, so he wouldn't change it. He thought he needed all the good luck he could find with a house and little sister to care for. Eli was hungry too, because Pop had sent him to bed without his supper. He dipped his hands in the basin on the wash bench and patted his face gingerly. How to get breakfast! That was the question. Always before, when it was time for breakfast, good crackling sounds came from the fireplace, where Mom had scrapple or sausage cooking on the trivet, and warmth came up the ladder to the loft. Now, there was just a spark of fire, and the early morning was frosty and cold. Sibilla cried for Mom.

"Don't cry, Sibby, I'll make up the fire, see if I don't." He went to the wood box and took out chips that he put on the embers a few at a time till there was a little blaze. Then small sticks, and finally "round" wood, round pieces with the bark still on. They made a good steady fire, Eli knew. Sibilla grew so interested she forgot to cry and picked up her little wooden doll from the floor.

"Now," said Eli, "it wonders me what we can make for breakfast." He had no idea how Mom made corn meal pudding. He did not know how to cook scrapple or sausage.

"Well," said he, "there's milk in the spring house and bread in the crock. We could have that. Stay here, Sibby, till I get it." Sibby looked as if she might cry again, but Eli shook his finger at her, and said:

58

"You know what Master Christopher says: 'Never are we alone.' And anyway, *I'm* here to take care of you." As he said that, he suddenly felt very brave, and Sibilla puckered up her chin and swallowed her tears.

Just as he was about to pick up the pitcher for milk, he heard a lowing from the barn.

"Why, that's Star," he said. "She hasn't been milked! What shall we do?" Mom always did the milking. Eli had only tried it once when he begged Mom to let him.

"Well, now, I *must* try. Mom says she must be milked every morning and night. Sibby, you can come with, but here's your shawl. It's cold. You must be quiet, so Star won't move fast and upset! The pigs we must feed too, and the geese."

Eli took the milk bucket instead of the pitcher and they went out to the log shed. He took down the milking stool. He filled a cup with grain from the feed box for the geese and handed it to Sibby, saying, "Take this to the goose pen and then let them loose."

"Come, Boss!" he said as he had heard Mom do when she wanted Star to move over. Her eyes looked enormous as he fastened the bar across to keep her in the stall. She mooed mournfully as if she knew that Eli was not the one to care for her. "It wonders me," he thought, "if she knows I'm the one that made her dance last night." Sibilla went off to feed the geese.

"Sibby," called Eli, "go once, now and throw down some hay. She's maybe hungry and will stand *so* if we feed her." Sibilla climbed to the loft and threw down the sweet-smelling hay. Eli set the stool in place and went to work. Star munched the hay but was uneasy at the strange hands milking her. No milk would come! Eli tried and tried. Then, he remembered how Mom said, "Gentle, you must be." All of a sudden milk spurted into the bucket. Eli was so excited he almost forgot to be gentle. The milk rang against the side of the bucket and soon it was filled. He carried the milk to the spring house, poured it into a pitcher, then turned Star out to pasture. Wouldn't Mom be glad he could milk! Sibilla clapped her hands and ran for a mug. Eli filled it and then one for himself. The warm milk felt good, and with bread, spread with new apple butter, was all the breakfast they needed.

The big clock struck nine. School time, Eli thought, and he wasn't there to read the Scriptures. He had other things to worry about. The wood box needed filling but first he must turn the pigs loose. When they went squealing into the woods Eli felt as if he and Sibby were alone in the world. Except for the little clearing Pop had made, the forest was all about them. To be sure it was only a mile or so to the nearest neighbor, but the trees were so high that not even the smoke from the chimney could be seen. Then usually, Mom could be heard singing somewhere about, or Pop could be heard cutting wood, but now there wasn't a sound except the crows cawing, and the dry leaves blowing in the wind. Eli believed what Master Christopher had said, "Never are we alone," but he *did* wish Pop or Mom would come home. Even Buck and Berry, the oxen, weren't home. They had drawn the load to market. Pop took things to market for several of the farmers who had no oxen. He took cheeses, rags for the paper mill, flax yarn to the stocking mill, and vegetables. In return the farmers gave fodder for the oxen and the cow.

Eli called Sibby to help fill the wood box, then he took the broom and swept up the chips that had fallen.

As he stood there in the silence, it came to Eli that there was still some work to do on the bench. He went into the shed and set to work with the piece of pumice stone that Pop had brought from Germany, rubbing the wood to a satin smoothness. He remembered then, that Pop was going to ask about trading the bench for window glass today in the German Town.

And the more he polished the wood the sadder he felt. He took the bench

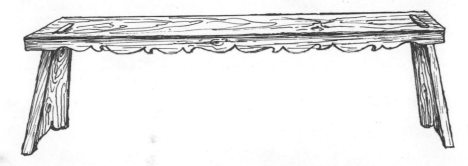

in and set it by the fireplace. It was just right, just what Mom wanted, and it really did look like the one they had left in Germany. He sat for a minute, enjoying it but thinking sadly too, that if he hadn't thrown that ball, Mom would be having it. How could he ever make up for his mischief? He wondered if Pop had found a place to sell or trade the bench. He half wished nobody would buy it, then he could leave it there for Mom. It looked so nice.

At last, he decided it must surely be noon, but when he looked at the clock, it was only halfway through the morning, so he went back to work at the flax brake. Sibby was happy with her doll playing in the leaves. Then she brought out her little rocker and played house. The frost had gone with the rising of the sun and the air was mild and pleasant.

Sibby began to be hungry again. Eli did wish Mom would come to cook dinner. He was hungry too.

The cupboard seemed to be almost bare, for it was baking day, so they ate more "butter bread." Sibilla took such big bites that her face was smeared with apple butter from ear to ear.

"Look, now," said Eli, "how your face is dirty? See how Mom's soft soap gives a clean face!" He held up the wet wash cloth. Sibilla shut her eyes tight and lifted up her face for Eli to wash. The door opened. Sibby waited for the wet cloth to touch her face, but Eli just stood with it in his hand. Sibby opened her eyes. Eli was staring at the door. Sibby turned to look too. There in the doorway stood *an Indian!*

"Ugh!" he grunted. "Me—White Eagle! Want food—hungry!" He rubbed his stomach round and round. Eli felt as if everything inside *his* stomach were going round and round. Then he saw the scar on White Eagle's cheek. It was the same Indian who had gone by on the road in the summer, and he remembered how Pop had said that the Indians of Pennsylvania were friendly and that a little food and kindness to them meant a great deal. So he answered as Master Christopher had taught him to do.

63

"Yes, Master White Eagle," and, putting down the wet cloth, went to look in the cupboard again. Sibby clung to Eli and tried to hide behind him but she didn't cry. There was only a small piece of shoo-fly pie, that Mom had made of molasses and spices, and some cold corn-meal mush, but White Eagle seemed to think it a feast. He ate it almost before Eli had time to put it before him. Then he sighed and drank in great gulps the milk Eli brought him. Sibby had crept behind the bed curtains and just peeked out, but Eli stood beside the table where White Eagle was. He looked at the shell earrings, at the strings of ermine hide hanging at each side of White Eagle's head, at the colored beads on his naked chest and the armlets. There was an eagle feather standing out at the back of his head and he had a great dignity about him. He had a sober yet friendly look and, when he saw Eli was without fear, he began to talk. He spread out his arms in a slow motion and said, "Land—White Eagle's one time; now white man's. White Man—my friend."

Then in his slow speech he told about his father, one of the Lenni-Lenape Tribe who had made the treaty with William Penn at Shackamaxon. How they had always kept the treaty. He made pictures for Eli to show how he made his mark. It was a white eagle in flight like this:

Finally he got up from the bench and said, "Now, me go. Go see White Chief for council. Go city of Onas, our brother, Penn."

He got up on his pony and rode away. While Eli watched him disappear into the woods, he saw Mom coming with the baby He ran to meet her and helped her carry the things she had taken to Katie Kreider's.

While Mom was putting away her things, Eli was telling her how they got breakfast, how Sibby had fed the geese, and how he had milked the cow so

he and Sibby had fresh milk for breakfast; about the visit of White Eagle and how hungry he and Sibby had been.

"Ach," said Mom, "what a big day it makes! This early morning I meant to come home, but so sick was Margareth I must stay by till she was better. Such a big boy you are so Mom could trust you. Yah well, the Good Book says, no one knows what a day may bring forth." She smoothed Eli's hair.

There were all the evening chores to be done: Star to be brought in and milked; the geese to be tended and the pigs brought in. Eli hurried out to the barn.

Just as Mom had supper nearly ready, they heard the wagon creaking through the wood and the slow tread of Buck and Berry.

"Just in time now," said Mom, as she lighted the candles. Eli helped Pop put the oxen up for the night and just as Mom called them for supper, someone else came riding through the wood clop! clop! on the dry earth. It was Master Christopher on his black horse, Firefly.

FTER SUPPER, Master Christopher said, "This is a fine solid bench I've been sitting on. It is well carved too. Would that be the bench you made, Eli? If it is, I'm sure that would sell in the German Town."

"Ach yes," said Pop. "I saw Master Casper Weimar today who buys glass in South Jersey. He said if the bench is well made it will pay for the glass. Next time I go to the German Town I take it and get the glass."

Eli couldn't say a word. His last hope was gone.

Mom glanced at him. "Yes, a good bench it is. Eli has worked hard. He should be proud that he can make such a good one to trade. For me, he can make another one. Maybe one Amos can help with to pay his share."

"Yes, Eli should be thankful too, that so soon the bench is finished," Master Christopher said. "We will be needing that window. And Eli has been a good boy today, too, I can see. I know now, why he didn't come to school when he was to read the Scriptures.

"Dear child," he turned to Eli, "maybe you would like to come with me to the German Town to school tomorrow? I have some errands to do as well. Some paper to buy at the paper mill and business at the printer's. Would you like to come?"

Would he! Eli could hardly believe his ears! Really *see* all the shops? Really stop in the market and perhaps go to the paper mill? It seemed too good to be true! Every time Master Christopher had gone to German Town Eli had wished he might go along.

Pop nodded, and Mom said, "Ach! Yah, you could go," as if she knew the trip would help him to forget the bench. Then Mom helped him tie his things in a bundle. He would have to stay the three days and could sleep at Cousin Jacob's fine house. It was hard for Eli to go to bed in the loft that night. Master Christopher slept on the settle before the fire.

They were up before daylight, and Mom had breakfast for them. She had cooked more corn-meal mush before going to bed, and it was ready to fry in the spider. Eli said he wasn't hungry, but Mom said, "It makes long till dinnertime, Eli. Eat once now."

The morning was fine when they set out, but chilly in the starlight before the dawn. Shadows were deep in the woods. As they rode through the trees, Eli held tight to the master who said: "The Book says, 'Thy word shall be a light unto my Path.' " Eli loved the smell of dry leaves, of smoke, as they passed a cabin, and of the wild grapes. He liked the sound of the horse's hoofs on the frosty road, that widened as they came to the village.

They rode through the wide marsh and on up the hill over the Bethlehem Road into the German Town. It was just about time for school when they drew up in front of the log meetinghouse where school was kept. The school looked different from the Skippack School. The benches had a back rail and faced the front of the room. Instead of a desk on the platform, Master Christopher had a table.

When noontime came the master said to Eli, "Go now, dear child, to thy Cousin Hannah's and let her know you are here. Tell her you may be a little late getting home this afternoon and do not linger on the way. You will have just time! You go down past the Market Square and on till you come to Grumblethorpe. Cousin Hannah's is just beyond."

Eli wanted to stop to see everything all along the German Town Road. Especially in the Market Square and at the Green Tree Inn, where the stable-boys were busy attending to travelers and a carriage which had arrived

from Philadelphia. But he had been told to be quick. So he hurried on.

Cousin Hannah made him very welcome and must hear from him all about the log house and how Barbara was growing. She had heard all the news from Pop only the day before, but she liked to hear Eli tell it.

"And me," he said, "I know my letters and can read!"

After dinner with Cousin Hannah and Cousin Jacob, Eli went back to school. The afternoon was much the same as the morning session. Reading, sums and a short time at singing.

When school was over, Master Christopher said, with a twinkle in his eye: "Eli, I must go to the mill for some paper to take back to the Skippack School. Would you want to go enough to help me sweep the schoolroom?"

Eli just grinned at the master and set to work. *Now* he knew why he'd been told to say he'd be late getting home! He made the dust fly so thick, Master Christopher began to cough.

"Not so fast, not so fast!" he said. "Do it *so!*" and he showed Eli how to draw the broom over the rough floor so the dust wouldn't fly.

Then off they went together.

The paper mill was so interesting! Eli watched the rags of old clothing go in at one end of the mill where they were cut in pieces. Then they went through the big vats that took out all the color, and through other great vats that dissolved the rags into a thick pulp. The pulp went through the huge vats, presses and rollers, then came out, at last, as beautiful creamy white paper with the Rittenhouse watermark upon it.

72

Master Rittenhouse gave Eli two or three sheets of the paper to take home. Eli thanked him—never before had he had any paper of his own. It would be fun to write on his own paper. "Perhaps," he thought, "if I make a journal and write about all the things I've seen in the German Town it will please Master Christopher."

By the time they left the paper mill, the sun was low, and it was beginning

to be very cool. Master Christopher put Eli before him on the horse to keep him warm. They rode up the Rittenhouse Lane and over to the German Town Road, down past the Market Square where the shops were closing, past the Friend's Meetinghouse, past the Green Tree Tavern, and to Cousin Hannah's. Candles were lighted, and Cousin Jacob was home.

They invited Master Christopher to have supper with them, and afterward sat talking before the fire until Eli fell asleep. Cousin Jacob picked him up gently and carried him to the little room under the eaves.

"School again on Friday," Eli wrote in his journal the next day. He had folded the paper into a little book and had already written about all that he had seen on Thursday.

Eli waited for Master Christopher again after school, for he had told Cousin Hannah he would take Eli with him to the printing office of Christopher Sauer.

The printing office was below the school and the Market Square, and there were all kinds of things to be seen on the way. There was the tannery, the Bringhurst coach works, the stocking mill and lots of shops and fine houses. But the Sauer Printing Shop that stood back of the house on the German Town Road was the most interesting of all.

Master Christopher Sauer greeted Master Christopher Dock warmly. They were great friends.

"And this is my little friend, Eli Shrawder," said the schoolmaster. "He would like to see how a book is made. We have seen how the paper is made at Rittenhouse's mill."

"To be sure, to be sure," said Master Sauer. He led the way to the little office. The desk was piled with papers, with almanacs, with bills, stuck on sharp pointed files and with several blocks on which were pictures cut into the wood.

Master Sauer saw Eli looking again and again at the wooden blocks on the desk. He picked one up and showed Eli how the picture was cut into the wood.

"You see," he said, "the man in the picture is using his left hand instead of his right hand, because when the picture is printed, it will be turned over like this." He showed Eli the print made from the block and explained how the ink was spread on the surface. Eli listened to every word and hated to leave the fascinating blocks. To cut designs in wood and see them printed would be even more exciting than carving a bench or a fan. But there was a smell of ink in the air and the sound of the press from the back room and he wanted to see what was going on there. First Master Sauer showed them the finished books.

Some were hymn books printed for the Mennonites, some were books of Psalms and one was a child's book. It was very small, just right for a child to hold, and it had two pictures in it. It had a very long title, *The Story of Little Gabriel, or the sin of Lying. Being a Moral Tale for the Instruction of the Young.* Eli wished he could have it, but books cost a great deal of money. Then he had another idea! It made him so excited, his scalp prickled. He didn't mention it, however, for perhaps it wouldn't work.

Master Sauer led them back to the pressroom. A man stood at a high bench sorting type and setting it in what he said was a "type stick." A boy apprentice, who was learning the trade of printing, was mixing ink. He said it was made of nutgall to make it black, gum arabic to make it hold together, and vinegar to thin it, so it would spread. Everywhere around the walls were pieces of paper tacked up, notices of news in the town, information to be put in the almanac, the signs of the zodiac and bits of decorations to put around borders and at the heads of the columns. Eli had never seen such a fascinating place. He longed to work the lever of the press and see the printed matter come out clean and bright.

Master Sauer must have seen how much he was interested, for he said: "Would you like to run this paper through the press?"

Even though he was so excited he remembered to answer as he had been taught. "Yes, Master Sauer, more than anything I would like it!" He eagerly reached for the lever.

"Vait! Vait!" said Master Sauer. "You must put the paper in *so*, with the

corner close against the mark. *Now—pull hard!*" Eli did pull hard, but Master Sauer had to help him. Then, Eli helped lift the paper carefully off the press. It turned out to be one sheet of the almanac. Each sheet was printed on both sides and folded into four so that it made eight pages. It had a picture on it too, for the title page and the signs of the zodiac to tell when it was time to make sauerkraut, when was the best time to cure hams, the best time to dig potatoes, and how to cure a cow of mooing for her calf.

"Now such a good printer's boy you have been, you shall have a copy of this almanac to take home to your father to read," Master Sauer said. Then he took Eli's sheet and put with it the one to complete the almanac, and gave it to Eli.

This time Eli was so happy he almost forgot to say "Thank you," but he caught Master Christopher's eye and remembered in time.

"Thank you, Master Sauer," he said, "I shall keep it always."

The next day was Saturday, but school was kept as usual. Eli lingered on the way, because there was so much to see in the Market Square. Farmers were weighing wagonloads of wood and of hay in the weigh-house. People were buying food in the food stalls, servants were carrying loaded baskets after their mistresses. Ladies in white kerchiefs and caps, gentlemen in knee breeches and buckled shoes greeted each other and passed, and the tavern yard was crowded with vehicles.

When noontime came, the Market Square was more crowded than ever. When Eli got here, he saw the reason. In the Square, right out in the open,

was a large round oaken table. Seated at the table and eating heartily were eight Indians! Waiting upon them, with great platters of food, were the women of the village. Even the women seemed to be enjoying it and there among the Indians was White Eagle, Eli's friend! Eli didn't go near; there were too many

strangers. But he watched for awhile, then went on his way to Cousin Hannah's. When he told her about the Indians feasting in the Market Square, she said:

"Ach yes! Whenever those Indians go through the German Town on their way to the Council in Philadelphia, they must have a feast here in the Square. But so! It keeps them good friends and never have they broken the Penn Treaty. Cousin Jacob says the settlers far West are having trouble with Indians. That is why they have the Council. We can be glad that no child need fear the Indians here!"

After dinner, Cousin Hannah sent him back to school, and the last afternoon session began.

My Son keep before and thine eyes God in thy heart

FTER SCHOOL Master Christopher took Eli first to his lodging place to get his things. There they mounted Firefly and went to Cousin Hannah's to bid her good-by and get Eli's bundle.

Cousin Hannah sent messages to Pop and Mom and some "sweets for the kinder," Sibilla and Barbara Ann. Eli climbed up on Firefly behind Master Christopher, and they started for home. It was still bright afternoon and perfect October weather.

They went up past the printing shop, through the Market Square again, and past the school. They passed the little stone building where the Lutheran School was kept and on out the German Town Road.

82

Down the big hill they went into the maple and oak forests blazing with color. Master Christopher began to sing, and Eli joined him. They kept time to the horse's hoofbeats, and he in turn kept time to the music, so they frisked along at a lively canter.

In about an hour, they came to the wide marsh again and to the Skippack Road, where the Farmer's Mill stood. Before long, the sun went down behind the hills. For awhile, the sky was a golden yellow, and the trees looked darker and darker till they were almost black. By the time they came to the Inden Hoffen Tavern the yellow had faded from the sky and the light was gone. When they reached the village Eli was so tired he fell asleep and would have fallen from the horse but Master Christopher caught him in time and set him before him so he shouldn't fall again. It was candlelight when they reached the cabin where Mom was standing in the door to meet them. She had heard the hoofbeats coming through the wood. Master Christopher helped Eli off the horse, then went on home.

Mom had a great kettle of pepper pot for supper, and Pop came in from the barn just as she was dishing it into the pewter bowls. The hot soup took the sleepiness away, and Eli began to tell about all the things he had seen in the German Town. He told about the Indians feasting in the Market Square, about the paper mill, and about the printing shop at Master Sauer's. That made him remember the almanac, and the sweets for Sibilla and for Barbara Ann, but he didn't tell them about the idea he had.

He had put the folded paper journal in his inside coat pocket, so he said

nothing about it but took it up to bed with him and laid it carefully on the candle shelf that jutted out from the wall. He wished he could get right at what he had in mind, but the next day was Sunday, and no unnecessary work could be done.

The animals must be cared for, of course, and simple food prepared, but most of the day was spent at the long preaching service in the meetinghouse by the school. Then after a dinner of cold food, Pop read the Scriptures aloud and they sang hymns. But all the while, Eli was thinking of his idea and how he would carry it out. At last it was time for the evening hymn, and the long day was over.

Very early Monday morning, while Eli was gathering the wood, he found a square piece that was just what he wanted. He hid it in the loft, so Mom wouldn't burn it by mistake. He didn't want to tell her what it was for. He wanted to see first whether he could work out his plan.

During school, Master Christopher said to him, "Eli, would you like to tell the boys and girls about all the things you saw in the German Town?"

But Eli said, "I am not quite ready yet, Sir."

"Very well, then," said Master Christopher, "perhaps Wednesday afternoon we shall hear it. Will you be ready then?" The teacher smiled. He knew that Eli must have some special reason for waiting to tell his story. He said, "You know if you do well these two days you are to read the Scriptures that day too, my boy."

"Yes, Master Christopher," said Eli. "And please could I have some of that ink you keep in the drawer?"

"Of course," said the teacher. "You must be working at home!"

Eli laughed but said only "Thank you," and tucked the paper of dry ink into his pocket. After school he hurried home to try something else he had just thought of.

When he got home Mom wondered what he was up to. He raced through the house, dropping his hat and book as he went up the ladder to the loft, then down and out to the shed, where he kept very busy, till Mom called him to help her.

Tuesday Eli could hardly wait for school to be over, so that he could get back to work on his surprise. He didn't wait for Amos or for Claus, but ran all the way home alone. He couldn't waste time playing until he had finished his surprise for Master Christopher. It was the most interesting thing he had done since the bench was finished.

As soon as he opened the door, he threw down his hat and horn book and went to the loft to find the precious journal and the special thing he was working on. Mom stopped her spinning and looked up as he came down the ladder.

"Shh!" she said with her finger to her lips. "What makes such a hurry?

Barbara Ann has just gone to sleep. And Sibby too sleeps on the bed."

"Mom," Eli whispered as he put the block of wood and the pages of the journal down on the table, "can I have an egg and some vinegar?"

"*Egg?*" said Mom. "What for? It is not the time for breakfast. And vinegar? What is it you are doing?"

"I need it for something; something *nice*. *Please* can I have it?"

Mom smiled. She got up from her wheel and opened the cupboard. She took one of the goose eggs from a bowl and gave it to Eli and poured some vinegar from the jug into a cup. He picked up two little doll-sized bowls from Sibby's play cupboard and broke the egg into them. The yolk in one bowl, the white in the other. Then he went to the dye kettle out in the open shed that Pop had built and dipped up some of the blue dye in a saucer. He went to the hearth and took a feather from the turkey wing brush.

Mom watched while he spread out all the things on the table beside the little book he had made, but she kept quiet. She thought to herself how much Eli was like her brother, how much he liked to make things. Eli went straight

to work. With his pocket knife, he scraped the feather down to a small brush. He mixed some of the vinegar with the powdered ink. The yolk of the egg was bright yellow. He mixed some of the blue dye with the egg yolk in another little dish to make green. It was just right! Then using the white of egg with the dye, he made a lovely glossy blue. Eli worked for a long time. Once he stopped to run out to the shed and came in with Pop's mallet.

Mom was so interested she forgot to spin. When he had done the best he could, he held what he had been making for Mom to see. "Ach!" she said, "so beautiful it iss!" She brought a needle threaded with yarn and showed Eli how to fasten the pages of the book together at the back.

When Wednesday came, Eli took pains to make his hair smooth and neat and put on the clean shirt Mom had ironed for him. He took the almanac from the wall and carried the little journal safely tucked between its leaves. He was in his place at school before Amos or Tobias had come in sight and had slid the almanac with the hidden journal into his desk.

The Scripture reading of the first Psalm went very well. Even the word "meditate" was not too much for Eli, but all day long he could hardly wait to show Master Christopher the journal and the secret he had made and to read to the children.

Finally, the arithmetic exercises were all finished, recess and dinnertime came and passed, and the girls had their reading lesson. Then the singing lesson came. Finally it was over. Master Christopher stood with his hands behind him and called on Eli to rise.

"So you are ready now, my boy, to tell us about the German Town? Let the children hear about it."

Eli took the little book from his desk. Everyone turned to look at him as he rose, and he suddenly felt very shy. Then he looked down at the little book. Should he show it to the teacher first or read it first? The boys and girls watched him expectantly, so he began to read all he had written.

The children listened closely. They didn't make a sound until Eli finished reading. Master Christopher, too, seemed to listen as if he had never seen all the things that Eli told about.

Eli closed the little book, smoothed the cover, and handed it to the teacher.

"This I made for you, Sir," he said. "It is not so fine as Master Sauer makes, but it was the best I could do. I hope you will like it."

Master Christopher took the book and looked at it in surprise. The cover had on it a picture printed in ink and decorated in color. It was a simple design of a flower and leaves but it looked very pretty.

"Ach!" said the master, "for *me?* Why, dear child, you have made a *wood block* and printed it on the cover! That is very well done. Even I have never made a wood block! You have colored it too! How did you ever get the colors?"

All the children turned eagerly toward the master to see what Eli had done. The Master held the book up so all could see. Then he asked Eli to tell just how he had done it.

Eli told how he had marked the outline of the picture first with a piece of charred stick on the block of wood, then carved out the design with his knife and Pop's small chisel. How he had mixed the ink with vinegar and printed the picture by pressing the block down on the paper and tapping it with Pop's mallet. He told about mixing the color with egg and dye, and then how Mom

had given him needle and thread and showed him how to sew the leaves together at the back. Everyone listened.

When he had finished Master Christopher said, "I shall keep this as a real treasure, my boy. Now," he said, reaching into the drawer of his desk, "I think you have really earned a present from me, and you shall have it." He brought out a beautiful painting with birds and flowers for decoration, a line of Scripture and the alphabet in both capitals and small letters.

A ripple of "Ahs!" went around the room as it was held up for the children to see.

Eli took it. "Oh, thank you, Master Christopher," he said. He thought it was the most beautiful one the master had made. He held the paper carefully till the benediction was said, then tucked it smoothly under his jacket and ran home as fast as he could go to show it to Mom. As he ran, he imagined how

nice it would look over the fireplace. He could make a carved frame for it.

Mom heard him running through the dry leaves and opened the door with Barbara on her arm and Sibilla peeping from behind her apron.

Eli held behind him the present from Master Christopher. He couldn't keep from chuckling, so Mom knew that he had a surprise for her.

"It wonders me now," she said. "What iss it that you have?" Eli couldn't wait any longer. He held out the picture and spread it on the table where the light shone on it. Together, Mom and Eli read it through and looked at all the decorations and beautiful colors.

"Ach, that iss fine," said Mom. "A good boy you have been to learn your letters and please Master Christopher."

"And, Mom," Eli burst out, "soon I will carve a frame for it. Then it can hang over the fireplace."

Mom nodded. "Nice that will be, but now we put it in a safe place." She went to get the great Family Bible. She smoothed the present carefully, to lay between the leaves until Eli could make the frame. Just where the Bible happened to open, was this verse: So Mom read it aloud: "THY WORD IS A LAMP UNTO MY FEET, AND A LIGHT UNTO MY PATH."